Galahad the Great

adapted by Maggie Testa
based on the screenplay "Mike the Knight and Galahad the Great" written by Anna Starkey

Simon Spotlight
New York London Toronto Sydney New Delhi

SIMON SPOTLIGHT

An imprint of Simon & Schuster Children's Publishing Division
1230 Avenue of the Americas, New York, New York 10020
© 2013 Hit (MTK) Limited. Mike the Knight™ and logo and
Be a Knight, Do It Right!™ are trademarks of Hit (MTK) Limited.
Nickelodeon and all related titles and logos are trademarks of
Viacom International Inc. All rights reserved, including the right of
reproduction in whole or in part in any form. SIMON SPOTLIGHT
and colophon are registered trademarks of Simon & Schuster, Inc.
For information about special discounts for bulk purchases,
please contact Simon & Schuster Special Sales at 1-866-506-1949
or business@simonandschuster.com.
Manufactured in the United States of America 0713 LAK
First Edition 10 9 8 7 6 5 4 3 2 1
ISBN 978-1-4424-5784-3
ISBN 978-1-4424-5785-0 (eBook)

Galahad is the
perfect knight's horse,
and Mike looks so
knightly upon him,
of course.
They're on their way now,
galloping here,
so as they ride in,
please give them a cheer!

Mike's mom had a postcard from Mike's dad, the king! "He wants to know how your horse training is going," said Queen Martha. "Why don't you show me in the arena this afternoon, so I can write back to him about how *very* knightly you are!"

"I'll start practicing now!" said Mike. "By the king's crown, I'm Mike the Knight, and my mission is to be the best horse trainer in all of Glendragon!"

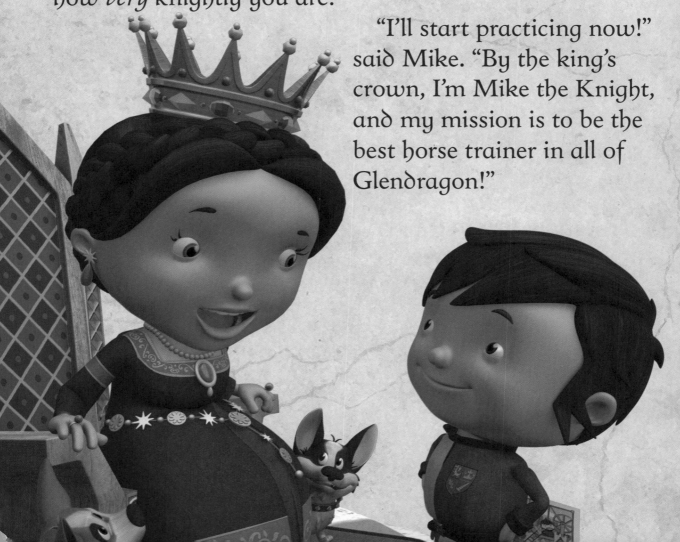

Mike put on his armor, opened a trapdoor, and slid down to the stables, landing right onto his trusty horse, Galahad.

"Huzzah!" he cried. Then he drew his sword, but found a golden goblet in its place. "I really wish Evie's magic would wear off! But I don't have time to worry about it. To the arena, Galahad!"

Mike rode Galahad around the arena. "I want Mom to tell Dad that my horse training is very knightly!" Mike explained to his dragon friends, Sparkie and Squirt.

"Let's see if I'm forgetting anything," he said, opening his training book. Galahad was great at Silent Sneaking, Great Galloping, and Tricky Trotting, but the horses in his training book were wearing fancier outfits.

At the blacksmith's shop, Mike found lots of new things
for Galahad to wear. "You'll look really good in these,"
Mike said, jingling some colorful—and noisy—ankle bells.

Galahad shook his head, but Mike didn't see him.

Then Mike noticed a colorful—and large—feather for
Galahad's helmet. He didn't realize that it flopped in
Galahad's eyes.

Mike's friends Sparkie and Squirt had fun shopping too. Sparkie found a big bow and a sparkly horseshoe necklace. Squirt found a purple bonnet and another sparkly horseshoe necklace.

"Now we're the greatest looking dragons in Glendragon!" Sparkie said proudly.

By the time they left the blacksmith's shop, Galahad had a new saddle, too. It was a very fancy—and very heavy—saddle. Galahad neighed and tried to tell Mike that he didn't like it, but Mike thought it was perfect.

"It's time to show Mom what we can do," said Mike. "Onward to the arena!"

Back at the arena, Evie set up a new obstacle course.
She laughed when she saw Galahad in his new outfit.
"Galahad, look at all that stuff you're wearing," she said.
Mike was proud of the way he had dressed up his horse.
"Now he's the best trained *and* best looking horse in all of
Glendragon. Come on, Galahad. Let's show Evie how well
I've trained you before Mom comes."

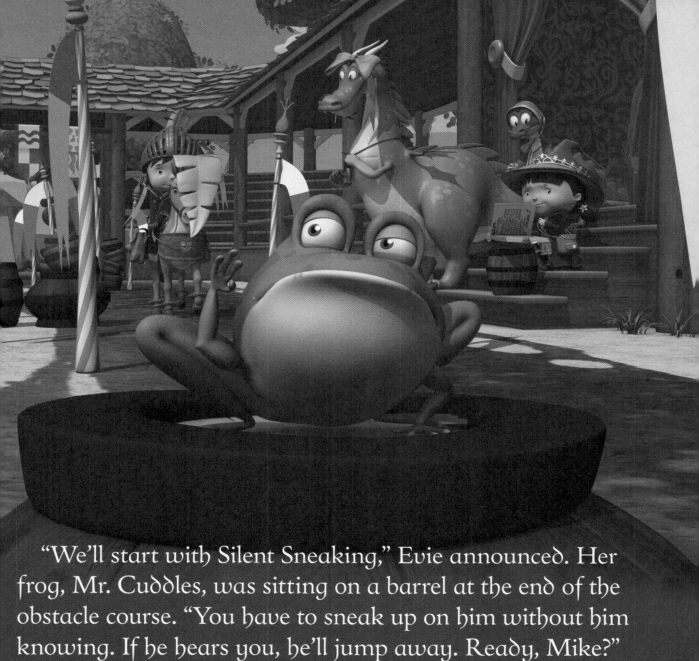

"We'll start with Silent Sneaking," Evie announced. Her frog, Mr. Cuddles, was sitting on a barrel at the end of the obstacle course. "You have to sneak up on him without him knowing. If he hears you, he'll jump away. Ready, Mike?"

"Ready," Mike called back.

Mike and Galahad began to sneak toward Mr. Cuddles, but it wasn't Silent Sneaking at all.

"Galahad," whispered Mike, "we have to be quiet!"

But Galahad couldn't help it. The bells on his ankles were jingling loudly. Mr. Cuddles could hear them. He hopped down off the barrel and over to Evie.

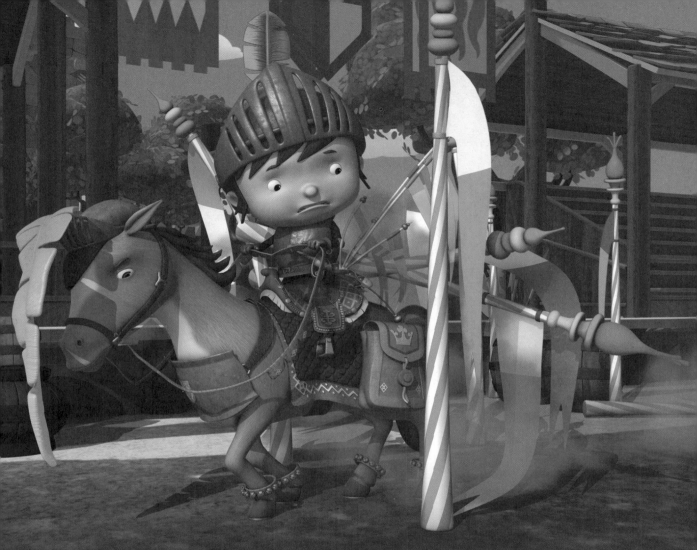

"Try the next one!" Evie called out. "Great Galloping. All you have to do is jump over the barrels and not hit any poles."

Mike and Galahad began to gallop, but because of the flags on Galahad's saddle, they hit every pole.

"Oh no, I can't look," said Squirt, hiding his face.

As they neared the finish, they got stuck between two poles.
"Oh no, Galahad!" cried Mike. "We're stuck!"
"Don't worry, Mike," called Sparkie.
"We're coming," added Squirt. "We're the greatest
looking *and* most helpful dragons in Glendragon."
Soon, Mike and Galahad were free, but Mike tumbled
to the ground. He wasn't feeling very knightly at all.

"The last test is Tricky Trotting," Evie called from the stands.

Before they started, Mike whispered to Galahad. "This is our last chance. We have to trot around the arena, then stop in front of Evie."

But when Galahad started trotting, he couldn't see where he was going because the feather kept flopping in his eyes.

Mike tried to steer Galahad over to Evie, but Galahad
stopped in his tracks. He took in a big breath. And then
another and another. He was about to sneeze!

"No, Galahad, don't sneeze!" cried Mike, but it was too late.
ACHOO! Galahad sneezed and Mike went flying!

"I'm the worst horse trainer ever," Mike moaned. "What
went wrong, Galahad?"

Galahad neighed and whinnied. Mike began to understand. "Is it the new stuff I got you?" he asked.

Galahad nodded.

"I'm really sorry, Galahad. I was just so excited about making you look great, but the bells were noisy, the flags got in the way, and the feather made you sneeze," said Mike.

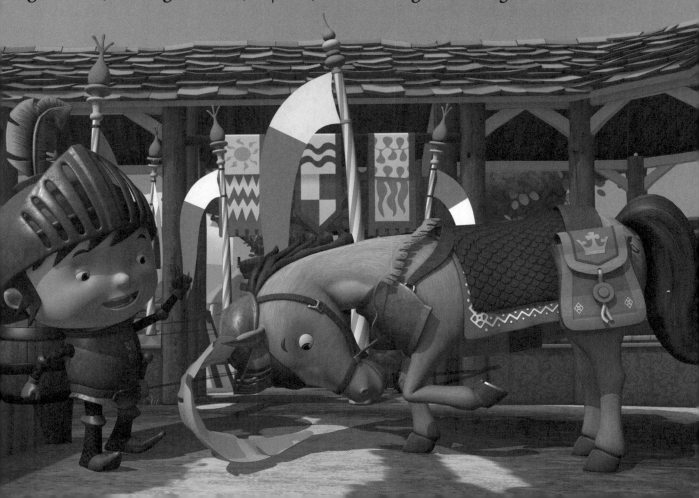

Mike was taking the new things off
of Galahad when his mother arrived.
"Hello, Mike," she greeted him. "Ready to show me
your horse training skills?"

Mike *was* ready. "It's time to be a knight and do it right!" he said and then jumped up on Galahad who was now wearing his regular saddle. There were no bells on his ankles or feather in his helmet.

"Go, Mike!" Sparkie cheered.

"Go, Galahad!" Squirt cheered.

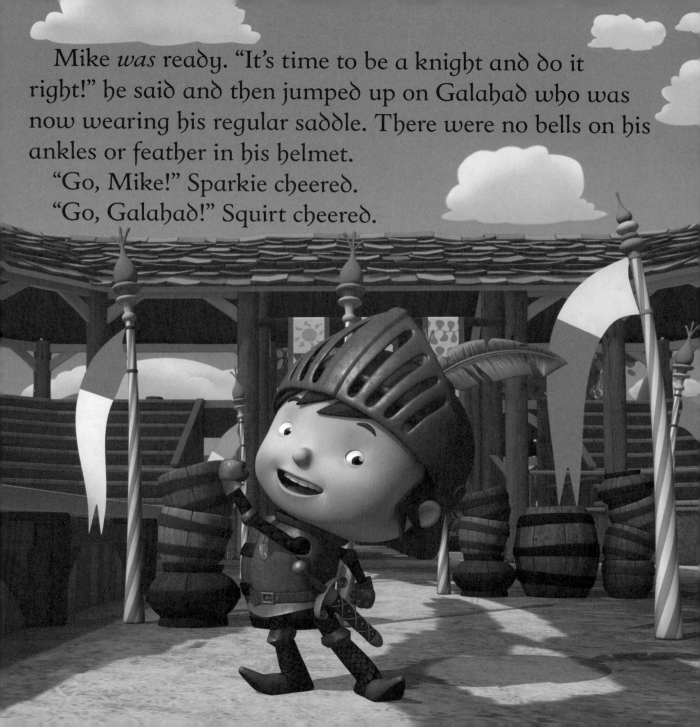

"Silent Sneaking first," Evie announced. This time, Mr. Cuddles the frog didn't hear jingling ankle bells as Mike and Galahad snuck up behind him. When Mike tapped Mr. Cuddles on the back, he hopped up in surprise. "Ha-ha! Gotcha!" Mike teased.

"Great Galloping next," said Evie. Again, Mike and Galahad completed the course with ease, jumping over every barrel and clearing every pole, now that Galahad wasn't wearing the fancy saddle.

"And finally, Tricky Trotting," said Evie. Mike and Galahad trotted up proudly to the queen. This time, Galahad didn't sneeze, because he didn't have a feather in his helmet.

"Huzzah!" cried Sparkie.
"Huzzah!" cried Squirt.
"Huzzah!" cried Evie.

Queen Martha was impressed. "Well done, Galahad and Mike! I shall write to your dad and tell him that your horse training is very knightly indeed! And I think Galahad looks rather wonderful."

Galahad neighed. He agreed!

Mike laughed. "You're right, Galahad. You look great just the way you are!"

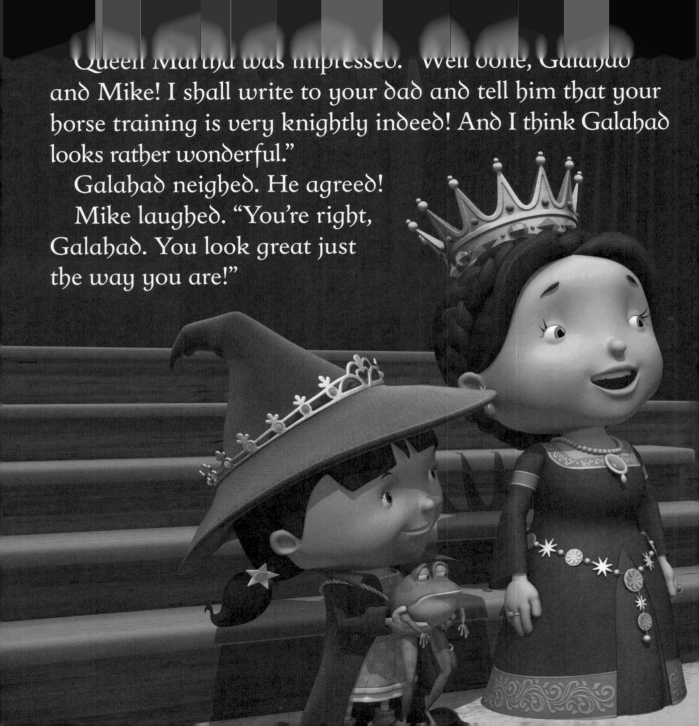

"I just wish I had a trophy for you," said Queen Martha. Mike had just the thing. He gave his mother the golden goblet.

"Perfect!" said the queen. "Mike, I award you this trophy cup for Knightly Horse Training. And for having the best horse in all of Glendragon!"

Galahad neighed happily and Mike chuckled.

Huzzah for Galahad the Great and Mike the Knight!